For
TOM *"Why do they have trees?"* BENJAMIN,
CLARE, SARAH, CONNIE, MATILDA & MILES

First published 2001
3 5 7 9 10 8 6 4 2
© Raymond Briggs 2001

Raymond Briggs has asserted his right under the
Copyright, Designs and Patents Act, 1988, to be
identified as the author and illustrator of this work

First published in the United Kingdom in 2001 by
Jonathan Cape
The Random House Group Limited
20 Vauxhall Bridge Road
London SW1V 2SA

The Random House Group Limited Reg. No. 954009
www.randomhouse.co.uk

A CIP catalogue record for this book
is available from The British Library

ISBN 0 224 04739 6

Printed in Singapore by Tien Wah Press (Pte) Ltd

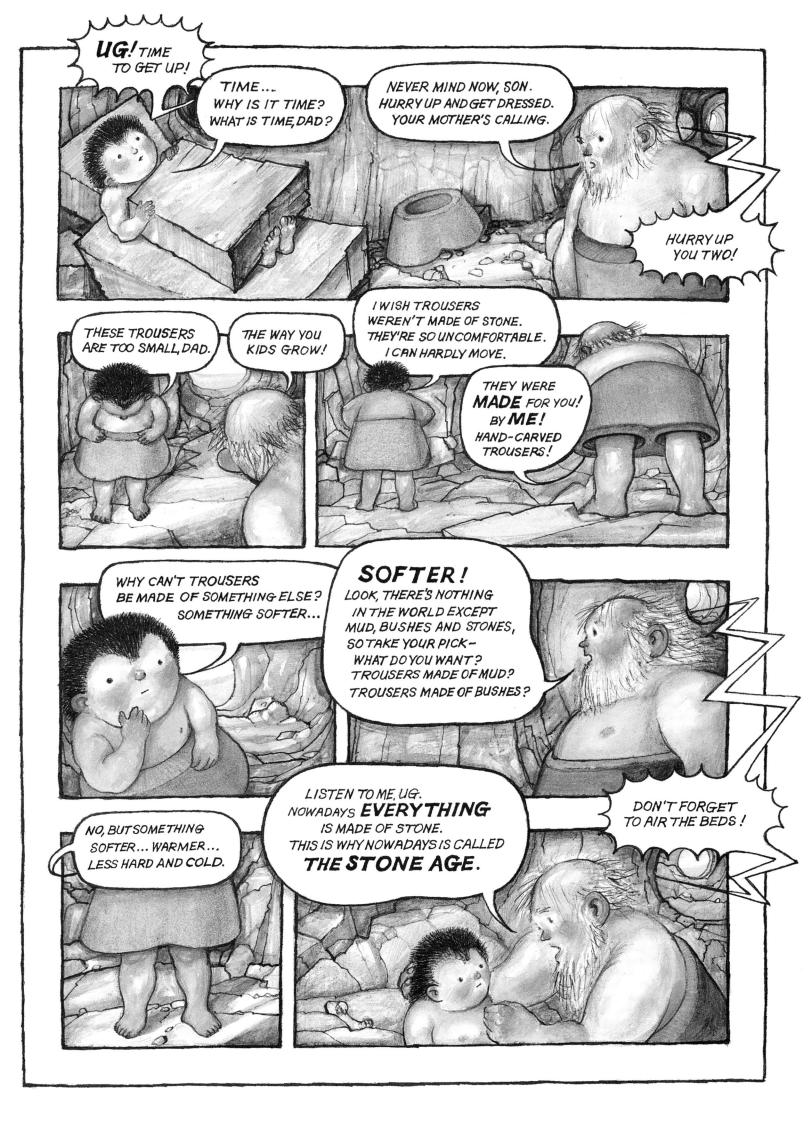

1. WRITE: (anachronism) IN THE STONE AGE PEOPLE COULD NOT READ OR WRITE. THIS IS WHY DUG'S SPELLING IS SO POOR.

2. IRON: (anachronism) IRON DID NOT EXIST IN THE STONE AGE. IRON WAS INVENTED IN THE IRON AGE WHICH CAME MUCH LATER: 4000000000000BC TO 20000000000 BC AND SO GAVE ITS NAME TO THE IRON AGE.

3. BUTTER: (anachronism) THERE WAS NO BUTTER IN THE STONE AGE. BUTTER IS COW'S MILK GONE SOLID AND TAME COWS DID NOT YET EXIST. THEY WERE STILL RUNNING WILD WITH THE PRE-HISTORIC MONSTER BULLS AND SO NO ONE COULD MILK THEM AND MAKE IT INTO BUTTER.

STONE AGE: (anachronism)
NO ONE LIVING IN
THE STONE AGE
WOULD KNOW HE WAS
LIVING IN THE STONE AGE.
HE WOULD BELIEVE HE WAS
LIVING IN THE MODERN AGE.
TODAY WE BELIEVE WE ARE
LIVING IN THE MODERN AGE.
TIME WILL TELL.

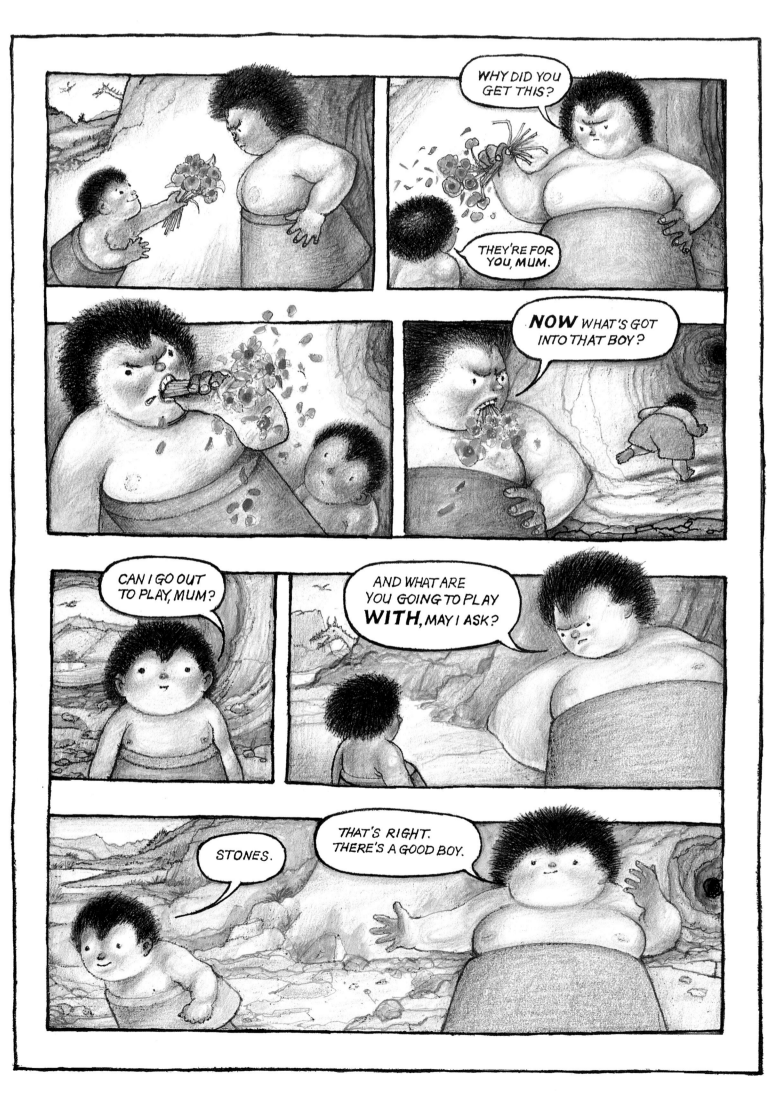

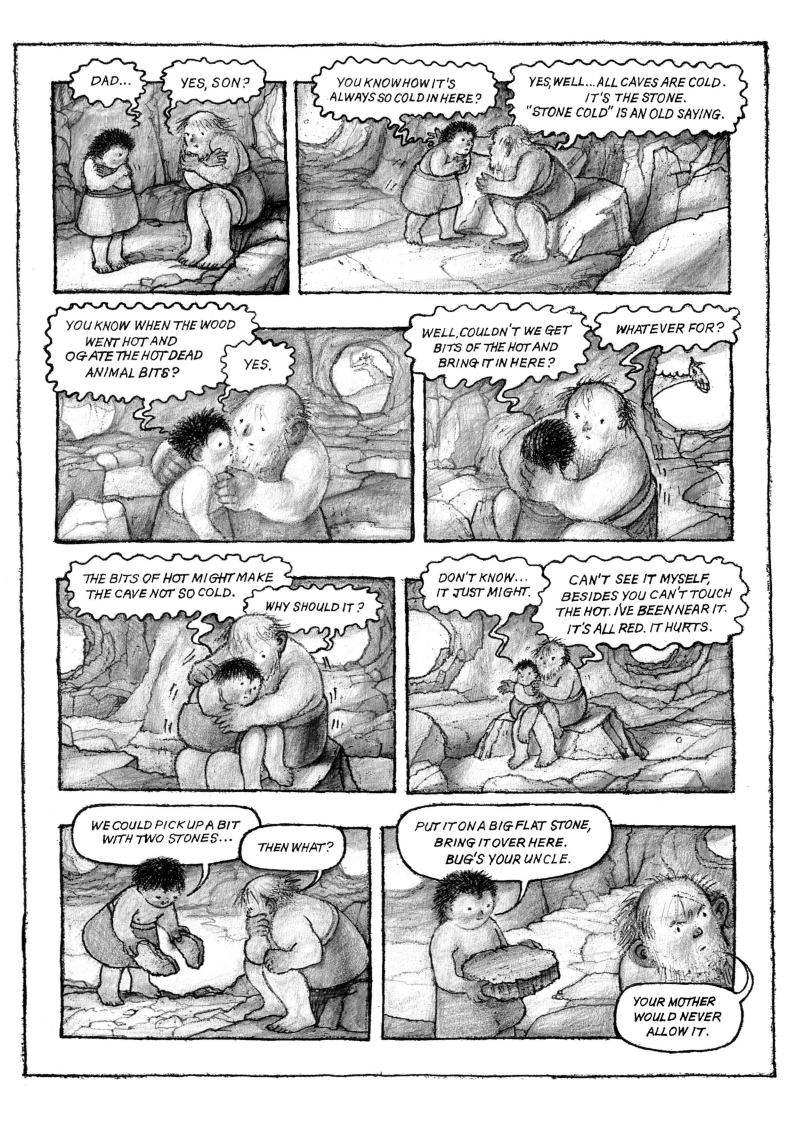

MUM...

HERE WE GO... YET AGAIN...

YES, UG?

WHY DO WE LIVE IN A CAVE?

NOW THERE'S A **DAFT** QUESTION IF EVER THERE WAS! WHERE ELSE DO YOU WANT TO LIVE? IN A **BUSH**?

IT'S SO HARD AND COLD AND DARK AND DAMP.

I DON'T KNOW! IT'S **MOAN, MOAN, MOAN,** ALL DAY LONG! "HARD" AND "COLD" WE'VE HAD BEFORE. NOW IT'S "**DARK**" AND "**DAMP**" AS WELL!

COULDN'T WE **MAKE** SOMETHING?

SOMETHING OUTDOORS, WITH A TOP, **LIKE** A CAVE, BUT OUTDOORS. WE COULD SEE OUT THE SIDES. YOU COULD HAVE HOLES IN THE SIDES. YOU CAN'T SEE OUT THE SIDES IN A CAVE.

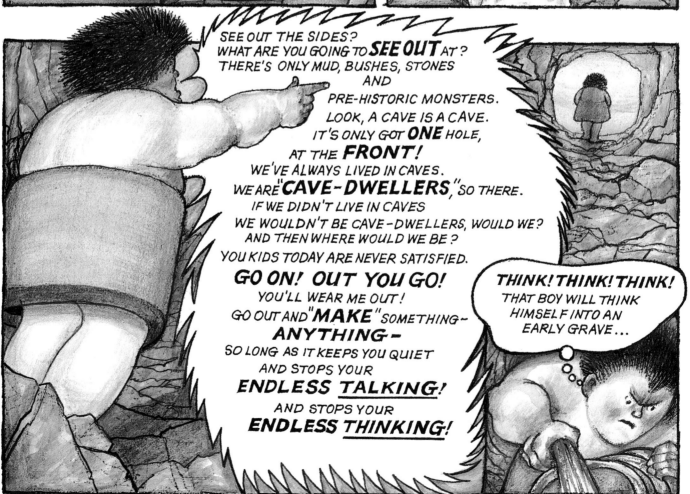

SEE OUT THE SIDES? WHAT ARE YOU GOING TO **SEE OUT** AT? THERE'S ONLY MUD, BUSHES, STONES AND PRE-HISTORIC MONSTERS. LOOK, A CAVE IS A CAVE. IT'S ONLY GOT **ONE** HOLE, AT THE **FRONT**! WE'VE ALWAYS LIVED IN CAVES. WE ARE "**CAVE-DWELLERS**," SO THERE. IF WE DIDN'T LIVE IN CAVES WE WOULDN'T BE CAVE-DWELLERS, WOULD WE? AND THEN WHERE WOULD WE BE? YOU KIDS TODAY ARE NEVER SATISFIED. **GO ON! OUT YOU GO!** YOU'LL WEAR ME OUT! GO OUT AND "**MAKE**" SOMETHING- ANYTHING- SO LONG AS IT KEEPS YOU QUIET AND STOPS YOUR **ENDLESS** <u>TALKING</u>! AND STOPS YOUR **ENDLESS** <u>THINKING</u>!

THINK! THINK! THINK! THAT BOY WILL THINK HIMSELF INTO AN EARLY GRAVE...

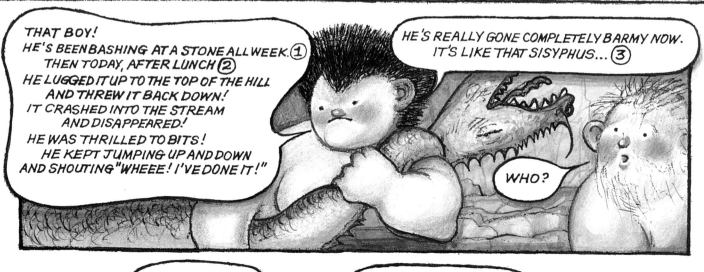
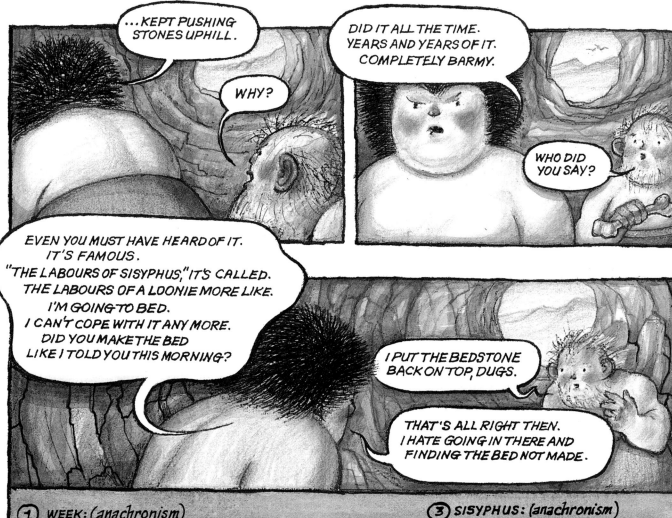

① WEEK: (anachronism)
THERE WERE NO "WEEKS" IN THE STONE AGE,
NOR WERE THERE "MONTHS" OR "YEARS."
IN THE STONE AGE, TIME STOOD STILL.
THIS IS WHY SO LITTLE PROGRESS WAS MADE
AND WHY IT TOOK AN AGE TO COME TO AN END.

② LUNCH: (possible anachronism)
IT IS NOT KNOWN FOR CERTAIN
WHAT THE MIDDAY MEAL WAS
CALLED IN THE STONE AGE.

③ SISYPHUS: (anachronism)
SISYPHUS CAME MUCH LATER,
AFTER HISTORY STARTED.
HE WAS A GREEK (OR A ROMAN)
AGES AGO (POSSIBLY EVEN BC).
HE PUSHED STONES UPHILL,
LET THEM ROLL DOWN AGAIN,
THEN PUSHED THEM UP AGAIN,
LET THEM ROLL DOWN, PUSHED
THEM UP AGAIN, LET THEM
ROLL DOWN, THEN PUSHED THEM
UP AGAIN. HE KEPT ON DOING
IT FOR YEARS, OVER AND OVER
AGAIN, FOR YEARS AND YEARS.
HE BECAME FAMOUS FOR DOING IT.

SO NOW IT'S **BOTH** OF YOU!
FIRST IT'S ALL **WARM, WARM, WARM,**
THEN IT'S ALL **SOFT, SOFT, SOFT,**
NOW IT'S ALL **NICE, NICE, NICE!**

WARM, SOFT, NICE!
PAH!

WHAT ARE YOU TWO GOING TO DO
IN THE ICE AGE, EH?
ANSWER ME THAT.
IT'S COMING YOU KNOW,
ANY MINUTE NOW.

DON'T SAY I DIDN'T WARN YOU.
DON'T COME WHINING TO ME
WHEN IT COMES.
IT'LL MAKE THIS STONE AGE
SEEM LIKE A SUMMER HOLIDAY. ②

YOU'LL HAVE TO BE TOUGH **THEN!**
TOUGH AS OLD BOOTS. ③

② SUMMER HOLIDAY: (anachronism)
SUMMER HOLIDAYS WERE UNKNOWN
IN THE STONE AGE.
ALTHOUGH NO ONE WENT TO WORK,
THE STRUGGLE FOR SURVIVAL WAS SO HARD,
DUE TO THE STONY CONDITIONS, THE MUD
AND THE ENORMOUS NUMBER OF BUSHES
THAT THERE WAS LITTLE TIME LEFT
FOR HOLIDAYS. SO THEY WERE UNKNOWN.
　FURTHERMORE, THE CLIMATE WAS
COMPLETELY DIFFERENT TO THE PRESENT
DAY AND "SUMMER" WAS PROBABLY
UNKNOWN DUE TO THE CLIMATE
BEING COMPLETELY DIFFERENT.

③ BOOTS: (anachronism)
BOOTS WERE ALMOST UNKNOWN IN THE
STONE AGE. ANIMALS WITH LEATHERY
SKINS HAD NOT YET EVOLVED, AS ALL
THE ANIMALS WERE STILL PRE-HISTORIC
MONSTERS. SUCH BOOTS AS DID EXIST
WERE MADE OF STONE AND WERE
ALMOST AS UNCOMFORTABLE AS THE
STONE TROUSERS. SO THEY WERE NEVER
USED. CONSEQUENTLY, NO STONE AGE
BOOT HAS EVER BEEN FOUND, AND
OF COURSE, NEVER A PAIR.